AIDEN

WOLVES OF THE RISING SUN #2

KENZIE COX

Published by Bayou Moon Press, LLC, 2015.

Aiden: WOLVES OF THE RISING SUN #2
First edition.

Written by Kenzie Cox.

Join the Packs of the Mating Season

The mating moon is rising...

Wherever that silver light touches, lone male werewolves are seized by the urge to find their mates. Join these six packs of growly alpha males (with six-packs!) as they seek out the smart, sassy women who are strong enough to claim them forever.

The "Mating Season" werewolf shifter novellas are brought to you by six authors following the adventures of six different packs. Each novella is the story of a mated pair (or trio!) with their Happily Ever After. Enjoy the run!

Learn more at thematingseason.com

Aiden: Wolves of the Rising Sun

She's the one woman he can't have…

Rayna Vincent has wanted Aiden Riveaux since she was sixteen years old. There's only one problem—he doesn't do relationships. So when he offers her a season of stolen nights with no strings attached, she accepts, willing to take him any way she can… even if she knows her heart will never survive.

Aiden Riveaux has a problem. A big one. He's sleeping with Rayna, his brother's best friend and the girl everyone thought of as his. Aiden knows he's has to break it off, but after one hot night everything's changed, including Rayna. Now she's his. And he intends to keep it that way… no matter what.

Sign up for Kenzie's newsletter at www.kenziecox.com. Do you prefer text messages? Sign up for text alerts! Just text SHIFTERSROCK to 24587 to register.

CHAPTER 1

RAYNA

"Meet me in the storage room," Aiden whispered in my ear as I leaned over the bar and picked up a round of drinks.

I paused and stared into his flashing green eyes. "I'm working."

"Aren't we all?" His lips twisted into that wicked smile that always made my stomach clench with anticipation. "All I need is two minutes, Ray."

I raised one eyebrow. "Wow. Two minutes. I'm not sure I'd be bragging about that."

He chuckled, the sound low and oh so sexy. Damn him. "Two minutes is plenty of time to—"

"Rub one out?" Luc, his brother and my best friend, slid up next to me.

"Luc, Jesus," I said choking on a bubble of laughter.

"You offering?" Aiden asked him, an irritated expression replacing his heated one.

"Hell no. Get me my usual. I have a couple of ladies to get back to." He nodded toward our friend Skye and her model friends sitting in a booth.

"Get it yourself," Aiden barked and slid down the bar to help a waiting customer.

"What's with him?" Luc asked me.

I shook my head, eyeing him. He had on black jeans, a dark green button-down shirt, and clean boots. He'd even put some sort of product in his dark hair to tame it into place. Someone was on the prowl tonight. "Maybe he doesn't feel like waiting on his little brother when the bar is packed."

Luc glanced around his family's bar known as Wolves of the Rising Sun, contemplating. "No. I don't think that's the problem. He's happiest when the cash register is overflowing."

That was true. The only time Aiden got upset was when someone was trying to stand between him and something that was his. Like the land, his family, the business… or whatever girl was his flavor of the week. I glanced over at the booth full of the sexy, voluptuous plus-sized models where Luc had been sitting for the past half hour, and the lightbulb went off—along with a sharp pang of jealousy. "He probably has his eye on one of them. Take the wrong one home tonight and he'll be moody for days."

Luc snorted. "It's mating season. I'm not planning on taking any of them home."

Right. I rolled my eyes. Luc had commitment issues just like all the Riveaux boys did. I'm sure some psychologist would trace it back to when their mother took off years ago.

I'd thought maybe things would change since the oldest of the three, Jace, had recently found someone. Skye. I'd hoped seeing him happy and mated would help the other two get over their bullshit and actually start dating as opposed to their notorious one-night stands. But apparently not during mating season, the one time of year they could actually become mated. It also explained why Aiden was suddenly showing interest in me. He wanted to scratch the itch without falling for someone.

"Well, just don't let me find you half-naked in the walk-in cooler again." I grabbed the tray and hustled over to my waiting table.

On my way back, I stopped to clear some glasses and watched as Luc sat down next to Skye. He smiled at her two friends, instantly catching their attention. How could he not with his clear blue eyes offset by his dark hair? He was every woman's fantasy. Except for mine. We'd been best friends since the first day of Miss Stacy's kindergarten class. He was the brother I'd never had.

I slipped into the kitchen to drop off the dirty glasses. On my way back to the bar, Aiden rounded the corner and grabbed my wrist. He pulled me into the storage room and kicked the door closed.

He pressed me up against the wall, one

hand clutching my hip as he ran his knuckles gently over my cheek. "You're killing me, Ray."

I raised a skeptical eyebrow, trying to ignore the way my heart was trying to beat out of my chest. "You look plenty alive to me."

"Not for long if I don't get you out of this skirt and your long legs wrapped around my waist."

Oh, God. Lust clouded my brain, and the memory of him fucking me on his kitchen table last week made me clutch at his black T-shirt. I stared up into his hungry gaze. "After work?"

"Now."

"But the bar," I said weakly.

"Jace can handle it." He dipped his head and caught my lower lip between his teeth, nibbled slightly, and then plunged his tongue into my mouth, taking whatever he wanted while I melted into him, ready to give in to whatever he demanded next.

Roughly, he tore his lips from mine and scraped his teeth down my neck to my cleavage.

"This top?" He cupped my breast, squeezing my nipple through the thin fabric. "You should wear this every damned day."

I sucked in a breath, silently vowing to do just that. It was a fitted, low-cut, wraparound jersey knit number that didn't leave much to the imagination. I'd worn it for the extra tips. Only now I was going to wear it for him.

Aiden lowered himself to his knees and pushed my skirt up. "Damn, why did it take me so long to notice you?"

Why indeed? My stomach did a little flip, but I instantly scolded myself for being sucked in by his words. This was temporary. Just until mating season was over. He'd made that perfectly clear last week before we ended up on that table.

Listen, Ray. I want you, but this can't be anything more than physical. You know that, right?

I'd heard him. Understood perfectly. And had all but ripped his shirt off anyway. I'd wanted Aiden Riveaux since I was fifteen years old. If this was my one and only chance to be with him, then I wasn't going to pass it up. Someday he was going to find his mate and he'd be gone. But until then, I was going to take whatever he was offering. I couldn't refuse. Didn't even want to. I'd enjoy today and worry about tomorrow later.

Placing one hand behind my knee, he carefully lifted my leg over his shoulder and ran his tongue up my inner thigh, making me shudder with anticipation.

Holy shit. Were we really going to do this right here in the storage room with all those people packed in the bar?

Both his hands ghosted over my hips. With a wolfish smile, he glanced up at me as his thumbs hooked into my panties, pulling them down just enough to bare myself to him. "I want to know you're wet and waiting for me while we're working tonight."

Wet? Mission accomplished. I was drenched and ready to climb on top of him right then and there. "Aiden, I—"

"Shh." He leaned in, burying his face between my legs as his tongue flicked over my clit.

"Oh," I moaned, pressing my hands against the wall.

His fingers dug into my flesh, and with a

growl, he scraped his teeth over me.

I gasped and dug my hands into his hair as fierce need took over.

"You like that." His words weren't a question.

"More," I demanded, everything pulsing.

His tongue laved my flesh once more, and then he pulled back, tugging my panties back into position.

"What are you doing?" I asked staring down at him, my eyes narrowed.

Releasing my leg, he set me back on my feet and stood up, searing me with his hot gaze. "We have to work, Ray."

"But—"

He pressed his finger to my lips and leaned in. "I told you, I wanted to know you're wet and ready for me. Because I want you so turned on when you walk through my front door that you're begging for me to slam into you, balls deep, right there in my entryway."

My mouth fell open.

He chuckled and covered my mouth with his, kissing me so thoroughly I was gasping when he pulled away. Smiling a secret smile, one he seemed to save just for me, he tucked an escaped lock of long dark hair behind my ear.

We stood there frozen, locked in the moment for a second as something tender passed between us. My heart did a dangerous flip in my chest, nearly bringing tears to my eyes. This thing, whatever it was, the emotions trying to suffocate me, wasn't allowed. I swallowed the unwanted feelings and put my game face on.

Aiden saw it and released me, backing up.

"Oh no you don't," I said and grabbed his

T-shirt, yanking him back. "We're not done yet."

His lips twitched. "Work calls, Ray."

"Just one more thing." I let go and took a small step forward, closing the distance between us. My breasts pressed into his chest as I feathered my fingers down the back of his neck. "I can't be the only one walking around like a ticking time bomb."

"Ray—"

I bit down on the hollow of his neck and pressed my hand to his already bulging erection. Moving up his neck, my tongue danced across his quickening pulse. Damn, the power I had over him, to know my presence had this effect, was almost more of a turn-on than having his mouth on me. If I didn't end this interlude soon, I was going to combust right there in the storage room.

I ran my palm up the length of him, pleased when his breath quickened. Moving my hand up, I teased his abdomen with my fingertips just above his belt buckle. "Tell me you want my lips on you."

He bent his head, moving in for a kiss, but I shook my head.

"No." I glanced down. "Tell me you want my lips wrapped around you."

"Rayna," he said, his voice hoarse.

I raised my gaze to his. "Say it."

He grabbed my hand with his and pressed it against his bulge once more. "I want to feel your tongue licking me from base to tip. And then, when I'm ready to lose control, take me in your hot mouth and torture me until all I can think about is fucking your brains out."

"Holy hell," I whispered and took a shaky step back, trying to get ahold of myself.

He gave me a cocky grin and said, "If you want to play this game with me, you better come prepared. See you out there."

Before I could say another word, he pulled the door open and disappeared.

I slumped against the wall, concentrating on breathing. Goddamn, that was hot. I glanced at my watch and groaned. Four hours until closing. I was never going to make it.

CHAPTER 2

AIDEN

"Hey, where the hell have you been?" Jace, my brother, demanded as I reached for the whiskey bottle.

Ignoring him, I poured a double, downed it, and then poured another. The warm liquid burned my throat, a welcome distraction from my aching cock. How I'd managed to leave Rayna in that storage room without finishing what I'd started, I'd never know. But I damn sure was paying for it now.

The second shot of whiskey went down

smoother and managed to take a bit of the edge off. At least enough to get back to work. Discarding my glass, I turned to help the next barfly but was intercepted by Jace.

He stood in front of me with his arms crossed over his chest, frowning. "I don't know what's got you all worked up, but you need to get it together. It feels like you're about five seconds from coming unglued."

I gave him a flat stare, resenting that he could sense my frustration. "I'm fine."

He raised both of his eyebrows, studying me. Then he frowned. "Who is she?"

"No one." I brushed past him. If Jace or Luc found out I was fucking around with Rayna, there'd be hell to pay. They both treated her like the sister we never had. I'd never seen her that way, though. At first she'd been Luc's annoying friend I'd never paid attention to. Then one day, almost overnight it seemed, she'd shown up on our porch wearing a short skirt and high heels with legs that went on for miles. I'd been dreaming about those legs ever since. And last week I'd finally given in to all that pent-up anticipation. Having her beneath me—

The door swung open behind me, illuminating the bar with the light from the kitchen. Rayna strode by Jace and me as if we weren't even there. But I knew better. She only ignored us when she had something to hide. The small, secret smile tugging at her lips told me everything I needed to know. She'd loved every minute of our time in the storage room. I stood back, watching as she leaned over Skye's table, clearing the bottles.

Luc glanced up at her and frowned. His lips

moved, and judging by the disapproving look on his face, he was berating her for something. But it couldn't be me. He didn't even know about our hookup. She'd made me promise to not tell him or anybody else and then threatened to castrate me if I couldn't keep my mouth shut. I'd kept my part of the bargain. Why wouldn't I?

But when he got up from the table, scowling, and stalked over to me, it was clear she must've told him herself. Dammit. I did not want to deal with this now. Not on our busiest night in three months.

I moved down the bar and turned my attention to the waiting patrons. After filling three orders, Luc finally found his way right in front of me. "Jesus, Aiden. What the hell is going on?"

Shrugging, I wiped the counter down. "Working?"

He huffed. "Is that what you call it? You and Rayna disappear for like twenty minutes, and when you two finally show your faces all you can say is you're working?"

"Look, Luc. You don't understand—"

"I understand perfectly." His eyes narrowed and his fingers bunched into fists. "Stay away from her, brother."

Leaning back against the counter, I crossed my arms over my chest and stared him down. "You claiming territory rights?"

"No. For fuck's sake. It's not like that between us and never has been. You know that." He glanced over his shoulder at Rayna. She had her hip out, balancing a tray of drinks while she spoke with Skye. "But I don't want you fucking with her head."

I ground my teeth together, his words piss-
ing me off. And the fact that they did made me
more than a little uncomfortable. On more than
one occasion I'd walked away from a woman I
found attractive because one of my brothers
was interested in her. But now? The thought of
blowing off Rayna just because Luc didn't want
me near her made me want to punch something... or someone. Namely Luc. "Rayna's a
grown woman, Luc. She can make her own
decisions."

"Not when it comes to this," he spat out,
leaning across the bar. His face was so close to
mine I could smell the stale beer on his breath.
"Don't even think about touching her, or you're
going to answer to my fist. Got it?"

Too late. I'd already had her, more than

once last week, and there was nothing that was going to stop me from taking her to bed after my shift. Luc was just going to have to deal with it. I was on the verge of telling him to fuck off when Rayna turned and smiled at us.

Her face lit up with pleasure, and it was all I could do to not jump over the bar and carry her off to my house right then and there.

"Goddammit." Luc brought his fist down hard on the counter.

The woman seated in the barstool next to him jumped and let out a yelp of surprise.

"If you have that big of a problem, maybe we should step outside," I said, fuming. It was one thing to not want me to hook up with his friend. It was entirely another to get so pissed off he was startling the customers.

"Stay away from her," he growled and

strode off back toward Skye's table.

"Girl trouble?" the woman Luc had startled asked, a sly smile on her face.

"Brother trouble." I forced myself to relax, stared her in the eye, and gave her my full attention. She was tall, maybe five ten, long dark hair, and bronzed skin. Exotic looking with big, soulful eyes. "You know, always the rivalry."

"Well…" She glanced over at Luc, her eyes flashing with mischief. "If you need someone to keep him, ah, occupied for a few hours, I'm willing to sacrifice a bit of my time."

I laughed. "That's entirely up to you. But either way, I'm sure he'll cool down on his own."

She gently bit her lower lip and raised her eyebrows. "Cooling down would be a shame. I rather like my men hot-blooded." She nodded toward Skye's table. "I'll be over there. Bring me a vodka and cranberry when you get a chance."

Then she sauntered over to the table full of models and stood next to Luc. After a few seconds, she slipped her arm around his waist and leaned in, whispering in his ear.

Luc pulled her in closer and laughed at something she said. Good. If anyone needed a night of debauchery with a gorgeous stranger, it was my brother Luc. He was always so serious, almost too careful about who he let into his inner circle. As far as I knew, he hadn't hooked up with anyone since the beginning of the year. He was always careful during mating season. Hell, so was I. Neither of us was in a hurry to be mated off.

Who wanted to be tied down in their prime? It was fine for Jace. He'd found Skye, the ex model turned photographer. And honestly, if she'd been my fated one, I'd have bitten her too. Because, damn, she *was* hot and cool to boot. Lucky bastard. Not everyone made out as well. Look at uncle Vin. His fated mate turned out to be Laverne Mayette, the destitute heir to the defunct Mayette sugar plantation. Talk about bitter. And now he was stuck with her and her family stories of the better days while they ate TV dinners on their front porch and argued over who was going to take the car in for service.

I shuddered involuntarily.

"Looks like she's got her hooks into him already," Rayna said.

I cut my gaze to the tall brunette standing to my right, and lust slammed into me all over again, nearly bringing me to my knees. Fuck me. I'd thought our night together would cure me of that insatiable itch, but it had only made it worse. Not that our interlude in the storage room had helped on that front. "Good thing you're coming home with me tonight," I said, scanning her body slowly from head to toe. "'Cause I bet Luc's already making a checklist of all the dirty things he's going to do with her—"

"Enough!" She held her hand up. "I do not need a vision of your brother getting sweaty trapped in my brain." A tiny shudder rippled through her. "Gross."

I laughed, feeling a bit of tension drain from my shoulders. There was never any question the two were just friends, but considering how close they were and that they shared a house… Well, I'd always sort of imagined they'd end up together. And I didn't like that one bit. Hated it, in fact.

"Whoa. What's that about?" Rayna reached up and brushed her thumb lightly across my brow. "You went from amused to pissed in about two seconds flat."

I stood there, paralyzed, not wanting to step away from her touch.

"Looks like a Hallmark moment," Jace said, suspicion clouding his voice as he wiped down the bar. "You aren't hitting on Luc's girl, are you?"

"I'm not Luc's girl," Rayna said defensively while I jerked back out of her reach.

Jace ignored her remark and leveled me with his stare.

I forced myself to hold his gaze while I grabbed a bottle of water. Keeping my tone uninterested, I said, "Headache. Rayna thinks her fingers are magic or something."

Jace glanced between us, shook his head, and then disappeared to the other end of the bar.

Rayna grabbed two bottles of beer, uncapped them, and said, "You're an ass."

My lips twitched.

"Make that an arrogant ass." With beer bottles in hand, she flung her long dark hair over her shoulder and sauntered over to her waiting customers, making sure to flaunt her perfect backside.

"Maybe, Ray," I said to myself. "But that's exactly what you like about me."

CHAPTER 3

RAYNA

DAMN AIDEN AND his perfectly chiseled jaw. Not to mention his six-pack abs, smoldering eyes, and the way he made me melt every time I so much as glanced at him. There was no way I was going to be able to keep this a secret from Luc. He was already eyeballing the two of us with enough suspicion to make even the most practiced liar confess her sins.

"What's going on with you two?" Luc demanded while he waited for Arianna, the exotic-looking model he'd been sweet-talking all night. She'd disappeared to the restroom. Everyone else had already left for the night except Aiden, Luc, and me.

"Nothing." I leaned over the table, gathering empty glasses.

"You're lying."

"And you're being a jerk." What was with the Riveaux boys tonight? Was Mercury in retrograde or something?

"So you admit it then." He sat back and crossed his arms over his chest.

I let out an exaggerated sigh and picked up the tray. "No, I'm not admitting anything. You're just fishing for information that's none of your damn business."

"Ray—"

"Hey, Luc, ready?" Arianna reappeared, her long black hair now tied into a sleek ponytail.

She cleared her throat. "Am I interrupting something?"

"No!" we both said at the same time.

Her dark eyes focused on me. "Looks like you two have history. Tell me if I'm getting in the middle of something."

I let out a huff of laughter. "Not in the slightest. Good old Luc here was just telling me who I can and can't date. Which is perplexing, because while he likes to tell me what to do, he is in fact neither my father or my keeper."

He threw up his hands. "Fine, Ray. Do whatever you want. I was just looking out for you. But when he stops talking to you or finds his…" He cut a quick glance at Arianna and shook his head. "Ah… I mean when he moves on, what happens then? Do you really want to see him every day after he breaks your heart?"

I gritted my teeth and sent him a flat stare. "He can't break something he can't reach."

"Oh, honey," Arianna said, placing her hand on my arm. Her eyes softened with a look of pity. "They have their ways." She eyed Luc. "The only way to have a no-strings-attached affair is to hook up with someone from out of town."

Luc rewarded her with a sly smile. "The perfect woman."

"Oh jeez." I picked up the tray and crossed the bar without saying another word.

"Here." Aiden placed a highball glass in front of me. "Looks like you could use this."

I dropped the tray, grabbed the vodka and tonic, and watched Luc guide Arianna out of the bar.

"Forget about him," Aiden said into my ear,

his warm breath sending a shiver down my spine.

Still staring at the door, I whispered, "Kiss me."

Since I wasn't facing him, I wasn't sure if he heard me. But then his hot lips pressed against my body where my shoulder met my neck. His tongue skimmed my skin as he worked his way up to just below my ear. "Is that what you wanted?"

I shook my head, downed my drink, and spun. His arms came around me, pulling me tight to his body. All thoughts of Luc and his warnings fled my mind. Reaching up, I buried my hands in his hair and pulled him down to meet my eager mouth.

"I want you. All of you."

He groaned and pulled back.

I swayed toward him, unable to stop my momentum.

"Whoa." His hands clasped around my shoulders, steadying me.

I shook him off, anger coiling in my gut. "I can't believe you. After that seduction scene in the storeroom and whatever this was"—I ran my fingers over my neck—"now you've decided to put the brakes on? Typical. I should've known better than to trust—"

"Hey." He took a step forward, eliminating all space between us. "I only pulled back because I don't want to start this here. When I kiss you next, I want you in my house where I can tear all your clothes off if I so desire. Despite the storage-room incident, I'm not taking you in the bar. You're too good for that."

The hard bubble of unease burst in my

chest, replaced by a happiness I rarely felt. A smile tugged at my lips. "Then what are we waiting for?"

Aiden glanced around the bar and grimaced. "Jace will kill us if we leave the place like this. And believe me, once we leave, we're not coming back until well into the afternoon tomorrow."

My pulse spiked, and I licked my lips as an image of us naked on his bed took up residence in my mind.

"Do that again and my resolve to wait is going to be nonexistent."

I almost darted my tongue out just to see if he was serious, but the hungry fire in his eyes was answer enough. Nudging my empty glass toward him, I said, "Then I'm going to need a refill or two in order to get through this."

"You got it."

By the time we'd finished closing down the bar, I'd sucked down three vodka tonics and was halfway through the fourth. My thoughts were slightly fuzzy, and a pleasant warmth had taken over my belly.

"Come on, gorgeous." Aiden slipped his arm around my waist. "Let's get you out of here."

I smiled up at him. "And into your shower."

His hand slipped down to cup my ass. "Not until after I make you come at least twice."

"Both can't happen at the same time?" I raised an eyebrow.

"We're not going to make it that far into my house."

Oh, lordy. I was in trouble. Still holding my drink, I sucked down the last of the alcohol, slammed the glass on one of the clean tables, and said, "Let's go."

"After you."

It took less than ten minutes to get to Aiden's house, but it felt like hours. He'd teased the sensitive skin of my inner thigh, caressing me the entire ride. By the time we pulled up in front of his small cottage, I was so wet, so ready, that I pulled him over to my side of the truck and climbed on top of him, straddling his legs.

Thunder rolled and seemed to reverberate through my body as I ground into him, his hard length hitting me in just the right spot. Moaning, I bit down on my lower lip and rocked against him.

"Rayna." His voice was throaty, full of need. Digging his fingers into my hips, he held me down against him and caught my lips with his own, his tongue thrusting into my mouth with such force, a bolt of desire shot straight to my core.

I matched his fervor, both of us lost in a lust haze, our hands clawing at each other's clothes. I barely heard the rip of my panties as he tore them off me.

Gasping for air during a quick reprieve, I made fast work of his button fly. He was bare beneath his jeans, making it easy to free his thick length. Wrapping my hand around the base, I inched closer, catching his tip right at my opening.

"Jesus," he said, his eyes closed.

I sank down on him, his cock inching into my sex, stretching me.

"Ray!" His hands gripped my hips, stopping me. "Not yet."

I shook my head and took him deep, letting him fill me up. "Now. I can't wait."

His hands stilled and he stared me in the eye. "We need protection."

I shook my head and moved against him. "I'm on the pill."

Wolves had superhealing abilities, and that went for diseases too. There was virtually zero chance of us catching anything from the other.

"Good," he growled and surged up to meet me, his hands tightening on my hips. Our movements were frantic, desperate. The tension we'd built earlier in the evening was too much to bear, and we both were lost to the fire consuming us.

He yanked me down hard and thrust up, filling me so full I thought I'd die of pleasure. But then he slowed, tilted his hips a bit more, and hit that perfect spot, the one that made all my muscles clench and my bones melt at the same time.

"Yes," I breathed, tilting my head back as I matched his pace.

His hands slid up my torso and under my tank top, one quickly freeing me from my bra. And the next thing I knew, his lips were clasped around my nipple, his teeth grazing the hardened peak.

I let out a low moan and arched into him.

"So fucking beautiful," he murmured and caught my other nipple between his fingers, squeezing at the same time he bit down on the other.

Everything tightened, and then suddenly an orgasm burst through me in hot ripples of ecstasy. I let out a loud gasp and held on, riding the wave while Aiden thrust faster and harder, his breath quickening with his own pleasure. I'd lost track of where we were or why, and all I felt was his hard, powerful body beneath me.

"Look at me," he said, his voice shallow and hoarse.

I opened my eyes and stared into his intense green gaze.

One hand tightened on my thigh while the other moved over my abdomen. His thumb pressed to my clit. He reared up and caught my mouth with his, drowning out my second cry of release with one of his own. We held still as our bodies shuddered together.

Aiden's head was buried against my shoulder, and when his breathing finally slowed, he said, "Damn, Ray. That's twice already."

"Huh?" I pulled back, smiling as I brushed

two fingers through his hair, loving the quiet moment we were sharing just as much as the incredible sex we'd just had.

"You came twice already. But I don't think I'm ready to take you to the shower yet." He cast his gaze down to my exposed nipple and blew gently. "There are a lot more dirty things I have planned before I'm willing to clean you up."

My breasts ached and my sex throbbed with his promise. Still joined, I tightened myself around him. "I'm ready."

He let out a low chuckle. "Just one of the many reasons I love fucking you. Insatiable." Brushing his lips across mine, he pulled my tank top down, covering my breasts, and gently lifted me off him. "But for what I have in mind, we're going to need a little more space."

For the first time, I noticed the rain pelting against the windows, and a chill swept over me from the shock of losing his body heat. I tugged down my skirt, trying to cover what I could.

Buttoning his jeans, he cast me a quick glance. "You okay?"

I nodded. "Just a little cold."

His irresistible lips twitched again. "Not for long." He pushed his door open, and it gave a loud squeak. A second later, he opened the passenger door and held out his hand. "Ready for round two?"

Yes. I was always going to be ready for him. Staring at his outstretched hand, I knew then I was in way over my head. Luc was right. When Aiden was done with me, when he found his mate, I'd never survive it. A small pain pierced my heart, almost making me clutch my chest.

I sucked in a breath. Not now. I'd have a meltdown later. Right then Aiden was waiting. I slipped my hand into his, and the moment his fingers closed over mine, all my trepidation fled.

Tonight all I wanted to do was live in the moment.

CHAPTER 4

AIDEN

RAINDROPS CLUNG TO Rayna's dark eye-
lashes. We'd gotten caught in a downpour
on the short walk from my truck to my front
door. Spring in southeast Louisiana was one
torrential thunderstorm after another. Not that
I was complaining. We stood in my kitchen,
each of us staring at the other. Rayna's white
tank top was soaked through, leaving her ample
breasts on display. Fucking gorgeous. I studied
her curves, committing the moment to
memory. When this was all over, I'd be replay-

ing the scene in my mind for years to come.

Leaning against the counter with one foot crossed at the ankle, I crooked a finger. "Come here."

She glanced over, a coy smile claiming her lips. "Is this where we christen the kitchen?"

I nodded.

She laughed and kicked her shoes off as she moved to stand in front of me. "I'm not doing anything until you get me a towel. I need to dry off."

"The hell you do." I grabbed her around the waist and lifted her onto my counter. "I've never seen anyone sexier than you are right now."

Surprise followed by pleasure lit her dark eyes as she glanced away, shyly shaking her head in denial.

Damn. Her reaction sucker punched me in the gut. I'd seen dozens of the townies hit on her at the bar, but that was just drunken bullshit. As far as I knew, she'd never had a steady boyfriend before. Sure, she'd dated, but she'd never tied herself down.

The urge to make her mine, to mark my territory, to *bite* her, hit me hard.

Shit!

Where had that come from?

"Aiden?" Rayna's brow furrowed. "What's wrong?"

The worry in her voice snapped me out of my self-induced panic, and I moved forward once again, inserting myself between her legs. I reached up, brushing a strand of wet hair off her cheek. "Nothing. Nothing at all."

"You sure?"

I lowered my voice and whispered, "One hundred percent sure."

Kissing my way down her neck, I ran my hands up her arms, warming her chilled skin.

"That's nice," she said softly.

"As nice as this?" I peeled her wet shirt off and cupped both of her breasts, caressing each nipple softly.

"Mmm," she breathed.

Everything about her was soft and smooth and luxurious. And suddenly I didn't want to take her there in my kitchen. I wanted her in my bed where I could savor every last inch of her. "Time for that shower."

She tilted her head to the side and gave me an odd look. "No christening the kitchen?"

I shook my head and lifted her off the counter. "Maybe later."

Her small hand felt so delicate in mine, making my wolf rise to the surface once more with the urge to protect her. From what, I wasn't sure. The only thing she needed to be wary of right then was me and what lurked inside.

Rayna slipped into the bathroom before I did and headed straight for the shower. With the water running, she turned to me. "This is a really nice space."

I glanced up at the open beam ceiling and then cast my gaze around the large room, complete with two-person shower and a separate spa tub.

"I bet the ladies fall for this every time." She tried to keep her tone light, but I knew her too well. That was irritation in her voice.

Using two fingers, I gently lifted her chin so

she had no choice but to meet my eyes. "The only lady I'm interested in is standing right here in front of me."

The frown lines around her mouth disappeared. "That's a nice thing to say."

"It's the truth."

She nodded. "I know."

It killed me that she knew about most of my other encounters. Hell, I'd picked up the majority of them at the bar while she'd been watching. But none of them were like this. None of them meant anything to me. Rayna was different. She was my friend first and lover second. And that's why this was going to get messy. But I just didn't care. I wanted her. Craved her. And didn't have the willpower to walk away.

Rayna stretched up and kissed the corner of

my mouth. She was so sweet, so tender, my heart squeezed in my chest, making it hard to breathe. Damn. That wasn't a good sign. After tonight, I'd have to cut this off. Go cold turkey. Maybe get out of town for a while to let this thing cool off.

Tomorrow.

Tonight I had plans. I flipped the water on, divested myself of my wet clothes, and then did the same for Rayna. She stood perfectly still, letting me do what I would.

But she wasn't passive. No. Her body was alive at my touch, just waiting for me to pleasure her. It would be so easy. I could take her right there against the shower wall with the hot water sluicing over us. My dick started to harden again with the thought of it.

She cast a quick glance down and smiled,

that secret smile I'd seen for the first time last week.

"Not yet, gorgeous. First you're going to let me take care of you." I tugged her into the shower, positioning her under the spray. "Hold still."

She stood there, confusion clouding her expression. "What are you up to?"

"What does it look like?" Holding her gaze, I poured shower gel into a wet cloth and ran it gently over her breasts.

She eyed the cloth for just a moment. Raising her gaze back to mine, she cleared her throat. "I thought this was just sex."

I froze for a second, not sure what to say. Then I shrugged, deciding to say nothing at all. She'd figure it out. "Turn around."

She hesitated, opened her mouth, but then

closed it and did as I asked.

Apparently we both knew words would only ruin what we'd started.

Neither of us talked while I took my time washing her hair and tending to her miraculous body. And when I was done, she tried to do the same for me, but I shook my head. "Tonight is about you."

She touched the soapy cloth to my chest. "But I want to."

I wrapped my hand around hers, stopping her. "No, Ray. Not this time." Not ever. I'd never survive her gentle touch. That intimacy was something I wanted more than anything, but couldn't let happen. Not if I was going to give her up. "For just this one night, let me put your pleasure before mine."

She shook her head. "Don't you always?"

"Not like this. Now go dry off and meet me

in the bed. I'll only be a minute."

Hesitating, she studied me. A small crease appeared on her brow as she frowned a little.

I bent my head and kissed her. Hard. Then gentled my lips against hers and whispered, "I want to worship you tonight."

A small pleased sigh escaped from her lips, sending my heart twisting. That sound would haunt me for months to come. I was sure of it.

"Okay." She kissed me and then stepped out of the shower. Glancing back, she cast her gaze down the length of my body. She took her time as if memorizing every last detail of my form. Finally she looked up. "Hurry."

I nearly jumped out of the shower and took her right there on the tile floor. Instead, I closed my eyes and hastily washed away the remnants of the day.

CHAPTER 5

RAYNA

WARM AND WRAPPED in one of Aiden's oversized bath sheets, I stepped into his neat bedroom. The coffee-colored walls went well with his dark-teal-and-chocolate-brown comforter. And the bedroom set... Damn, it was gorgeous. A distressed oak armoire sat against the far wall. Two matching nightstands with ebony surfaces flanked each side of the bed. And to tie it all together was an ornate espresso dresser with carved scrollwork. Had he decorated it himself? It didn't have a feminine touch, but it didn't scream bachelor either.

It didn't matter. I knew Aiden wasn't seeing anyone but me right then. He might get around and was a giant flirt, but he was honest. And loyal. And he wanted me.

A tingle of anticipation fluttered in my stomach. Dropping the towel to the floor, I climbed onto his bed, lay back, and waited. Air from the slow-moving ceiling fan caressed my skin, and I closed my eyes, pretending it was Aiden running his fingers over me.

My nipples tightened and an ache built between my thighs. "Hurry," I whispered, eyeing the bathroom door. But the water was still running. I'd never last.

With Aiden's wet body still burned in my memory, I inched my hand down my stomach, stopping at the swell of my mound. A wicked thrill shot through me at the thought of touching myself while he was just on the other side of the door. Biting my lip, I dug my fingernails into my skin, waiting.

The water shut off, and moments later, Aiden pulled the door open. He took two steps and paused, his gaze sweeping over me. His muscles tensed as he clutched the door frame.

God, he was sexy, standing there, his towel hanging low on his hips.

"Ray?" His voice was hoarse, thick with desire.

I stared him straight in the eye. "Tell me what you want me to do."

He shook his head, but his gaze shifted to my hand, which was poised to dip between my thighs. Clearing his throat, he said, "I thought

I'd be the one doing things for you."

"No. Not yet." And then with him standing there watching me, I bent one knee and flattened my foot against the bed, giving myself better access as I slipped one finger between my already slick folds.

"Oh, Jesus," Aiden murmured, standing perfectly still.

I sent him a small self-satisfied smile and dipped into my center, my hips jerking involuntarily with my touch.

Aiden's expression turned dark. A storm brewed in his eyes as he watched with rapt attention.

A surge of power overtook me, and I realized that when it came to sex with Aiden, this was the first time I was truly in control. He was mine to command. I loved it, was drunk on the knowledge of it. "Drop your towel," I ordered.

Keeping his eyes glued to my body, he yanked the towel off and let it fall at his feet.

Goddamn, he was glorious. His erection was bigger than I remembered, and I licked my lips, thinking of tasting him. "Touch yourself."

"No." He shook his head.

"Yes. For me."

"Rayna." He groaned and slipped his hand over his cock, holding it at the base. "You're killing me."

"Just like that," I said and let out a little gasp as I pressed my thumb to my clit. The torture of watching him grow even larger while I pleasured myself was deliciously naughty, spiking my arousal to new heights. I wanted him inside me, wanted him to overpower me, to just take me. Wanted him out of control and wild.

Wanted his wolf.

My tongue darted out, touching my upper lip as I rocked against my fingers, the pressure in my core building.

Aiden was still and silent, his body rigid and ready to pounce.

"How much do you want me?" I whispered.

"So fucking much," he answered, his breath ragged, "that when I finally get inside you, I'm never going to want to leave."

That's what I was counting on.

I lifted my hips, grinding against my fingers, and just before I came, I pulled my hand away and clutched at the comforter. "Now, Aiden."

He pounced. In one leap, he was on the bed, his head between my thighs, his hot breath blowing against my sex.

"Now," I demanded again, writhing in need.

He slipped his arms under my legs and wrapped his hands around my thighs, pulling them wider. Then his tongue was on me, tasting, teasing, torturing.

"Oh, God," I gasped, my muscles tightening as the pressure built.

He redoubled his efforts, quickening the pace of his greedy tongue.

I bit down hard on my lower lip and threw my head back. I was right on the verge of losing myself to the most epic orgasm when he pulled back and stared down at me, his eyes gleaming.

"What are you…?" I shook my head. "Don't stop now."

The corners of his mouth turned up into a ghost of a smile. "Relax, gorgeous. I'll take you there. Eventually."

Oh, fuck. This was payback for the masturbation seduction.

He was going to make me suffer. And it only turned me on more. I lifted myself up on my elbows and nipped at his lower lip, tasting myself on him.

Wrapping one arm around my back, he held me to him and kissed me so thoroughly my head was swimming by the time he laid me back down.

Every part of me ached for his touch. "Aiden," I begged.

He answered by dipping his head and taking one nipple between his teeth and plunging his fingers between my legs.

I gasped and let out a cry of both pleasure and pain.

He paused and withdrew. "You okay?"

I nodded and almost whimpered. "More."

"You like it rough?" he asked, raising one eyebrow.

Closing my eyes, I nodded again.

"You want that now?"

My eyes flew open. He was poised above me, supporting himself with both hands, only our thighs brushing against each other. I reached up and pulled him down so that I could scrape my teeth along his neck. Then I whispered, "Yes. Rough. Take me hard and don't stop until I'm screaming your name."

Heat burned my cheeks as I confessed my true desires for the first time. I'd been with a handful of men, but never any I trusted the way I trusted Aiden.

His gaze bore into mine as he appeared to

process what I'd just said.

"Please, Aiden," I said, thankful my voice didn't shake with my nerves trying to take over.

He bent his head and kissed me softly; then without warning, he grabbed both of my wrists, positioned them over my head, and pressed them into the bed, leaving me no opportunity to escape. "You're mine now," he growled.

"Yours," I agreed and rose to meet him as he slammed into me, burying himself deep. He gave me no reprieve, pulling out and pounding back into me so hard, pleasure and pain rippled up my spine. I let out a cry, but Aiden swallowed it with his demanding kiss.

When he broke free, he lifted one of my legs higher, positioning it over his shoulder. Then he grabbed hold of my hips and held me still as he fucked me, his eyes wild and chest glistening with sweat.

Every part of me was alive, reveling in the way he used me for his own pleasure. Loving the way I brought the animal out in him. Saw what I always knew was beneath his surface.

Holding me to him, his grip tightened around my waist and he leaned over me, whispering, "Is this what you want, Ray? For me to fuck you blind? Until you're ruined for any other man?" His words were full of seduction.

"Yes," I whimpered, writhing against him, needing for him to finish what he'd started.

He let out a low laugh, sucked hard on my nipple, and drove into me, taking every bit I was willing to give. His movements were slow and deliberate and torturous.

It was perfect. He was perfect.

"Touch yourself, Rayna," he ordered between thrusts.

I didn't hesitate. Both hands moved up to my breasts, my fingers closing over my nipples.

He jerked his hips, and I moaned as he pulled out to his tip. "Good. Now pinch them both. Make them hard for me."

"I will, just as soon as you give me more of what I want."

His fingers dug into my hips, and as he moved, I clamped down on my nipples and let out a cry of ecstasy.

Aiden paused as I pulsed around him. Our eyes met, and in that moment, the control we'd both barely maintained shattered.

Groaning, he let go of my hips and leaned over me, his teeth scraping down my neck. I clawed at his back, wrapped my legs around his hips, and met his frantic pace, both of us out of our minds with the need for release.

Everything around us stopped. All I knew was sensation and love and pleasure. He was the only man I wanted. The only one I'd ever wanted. All rational thought fled from my mind, and when the dam burst and the wave started to take me under its spell, I said, "Bite me, Aiden. Make me yours forever."

CHAPTER 6

AIDEN

M Y WOLF WAS right there. Ready to take her. Had been since we'd first started this game of rough seduction. It had taken all my willpower to not bite her the moment I'd walked out of the shower and she'd touched herself for me.

Mine.

And now she was offering herself. I should have stopped loving her. Because it wasn't fucking anymore. I needed her. Felt her deep in my soul, calling to me and my wolf.

"Oh God, oh God," she said, gasping, clenching her sex around me. "Do it. Bite me."

I was powerless to say no. The wolf took over. After one last forceful thrust of my hips, my teeth tore into her shoulder.

A low moan escaped from deep in her throat. And suddenly she reared up and cried out, her body convulsing with a powerful orgasm. Only then did I feel the tightening of my balls as I spilled into her, my own ecstasy taking me to a place of pure bliss.

Afterward, we lay there, completely still, my head buried against her neck as she clung to me. I stared at the wolf bite in fascination, watching it heal right before my eyes.

In awe, I stroked my thumb over her delicate skin and felt pride well up from deep in my soul.

Mate.

I bolted upright and stared down at her in horror.

"Aiden? What's wrong?" she asked, her eyes still soft with the contentment of mind-blowing sex. Or was she still dazed from my wolf bite?

"Shit," I muttered. What had I done?

CHAPTER 7

RAYNA

P AIN HAD RUPTURED through my shoulder with Aiden's bite, followed immediately by the most intense orgasm of my life. I'd all but come apart beneath him, felt as if I'd shattered and then been glued back together. I was boneless, sated, content.

Or I was until Aiden shot up out of bed and started cursing under his breath.

Fear clogged my throat. I hadn't been totally myself when I'd demanded that Aiden bite me. Asking a were to make you his mate while having really great sex was all kinds of wrong. It was the equivalent of pronouncing love right before an orgasm. Terrible idea.

Now he was stuck with me as his mate. And clearly regretting it.

"Son of a… Dammit, Aiden. I'm sorry." I rolled out of his bed and grabbed my discarded bath sheet, hastily covering myself. "I'll get dressed and be out of here in a few minutes."

"Huh?" Aiden glanced up at me in confusion.

I took one look at his beautiful face and bolted for the bathroom door.

"Rayna!" he called.

My stomach rolled with nausea and my head swam, most likely a side effect of his bite. But I didn't stop until I was in the bathroom, the door shut behind me. Only then did I let the tears burning the back of my eyes fall.

"Ray?" Aiden's voice carried through the door.

I flinched and leaned against the tiled wall, holding my forehead with my hand. My temple pulsed with a low-grade headache. It was definitely the wolf bite that was the culprit. When a new wolf was turned, it wasn't unusual to experience flu-like symptoms for a few days.

"Are you all right?"

I nodded even though he couldn't see me. Maybe I was trying to reassure myself. "Fine," I said and then added, "I just need a minute."

Silence.

I knew he was still there. I could smell him. Soap and sex and his natural woodsy scent mixed together and made my gut twist. All I wanted to do was open the door and wrap myself around him. But I couldn't do that. Not now. Maybe not ever. Not if he regretted biting me.

Straightening my shoulders, I held my head high and said, "I'm going to take a quick shower and then be right out."

"Open the door, Ray." His words weren't a request.

"Everything's fine. I swear." Reaching into the shower, I turned the water on.

A frustrated growl rumbled from the other side of the door, followed by the rattling of the handle.

I pretended not to notice and climbed into the shower. I'd just picked up the shower gel when I heard a loud crash followed by Aiden nearly ripping the shower curtain off the rod.

"Hey!" I said.

He stepped into the shower, pulled me into his arms, and nuzzled my shoulder where he'd bitten me. "Now, one more time. Are you all right?"

The tension drained from me with his touch. "I think so. Just a little dizzy."

"It's the bite," he said, running his fingers through my hair.

I nodded.

"About that—"

I held my hand up, stopping him. My emotions were running so high that if I let him finish, I was likely to burst into tears. I needed some time to settle. "Can we talk about this a little later?"

He studied me for a moment. Then he pressed a soft kiss to my forehead. "Sure, gorgeous."

I nodded once and turned to rinse my chest and torso. Aiden reached for the body wash but stilled suddenly.

A second later, we heard a commotion from the front of the house. "Aiden?" a familiar male voice called. "Get your ass out here."

"What the hell?" he muttered.

"It's Luc." Damn, what was he doing here in the middle of the night? I thought he'd be passed out next to Arianna by now.

"Fuck." Aiden stepped out of the shower and disappeared into his bedroom.

I stood under the water, not wanting to be a part of whatever conversation they were having. Hopefully Luc would assume I was some local Aiden had picked up after hours. He could not know I was here. We'd never hear the end of it. I wasn't ready for the lectures just yet.

"Rayna!" Luc bellowed from what had to be just outside the bathroom door. "Get dressed. It's time to go."

"Go away. I'll come home when I feel like it." I turned the water off and reached for a fresh towel.

"Dammit, Ray. I'm not fucking around. Just do as I say. And hurry."

The door cracked open, and I tightened the towel around me. "Do not come in here. I'm not dressed!"

"It's me," Aiden said. Then he disappeared behind the door again and lowered his voice as he spoke to Luc. "Wait for us in the living room."

"I'm not going anywhere. And you can stay the fuck away from her. Rayna!"

I stalked over to the door and pulled it

open.

Luc had a fistful of Aiden's T-shirt in his hand and was leaning in, a murderous expression on his face. Aiden just stood there, holding the clothes I'd left on the floor in the kitchen.

I gritted my teeth and took my clothes from Aiden. "I'll be out in a minute. Try not to kill each other."

Luc turned his glare on me. "What the fuck were you thinking, jumping into his bed?"

I stared him down, my eyes narrowed. Then, without a word, I slammed the door in his face. I'd had just about enough of the Riveaux brothers. Leaning against the door, I clutched my clothes to my chest and fought the urge to punch something. Namely Luc.

"Talk to my mate that way again, and you'll be looking at a couple of black eyes. Got it?" I heard Aiden say through the door.

Luc grunted. Heavy footsteps sounded on the hardwood floors, followed by the slamming of a door.

A soft knock came from the bedroom. "Ray? It's me again," Aiden said.

I took a deep breath and opened the door.

"Something has happened. I need to take you to Jace and Skye's place while we deal with it." Anger colored his tone, but more than that, there was worry. This wasn't just about Luc finding out we were together.

"What is it? Jace?"

"There's been a fire at the bar."

"Oh my god! Is it still burning?"

He shook his head. "I don't know. The fire-fighters are there. But, Ray, when Jace and Skye got there, Skye saw someone that could be connected with the Hunters. We have to go track the bastard down."

I hastily pulled my clothes on. "All right. Let's go."

Aiden put his hand on the small of my back and guided me outside to Luc's truck where he was waiting for us.

I climbed in and sat there, wedged between them both, more uncomfortable than if I were on display in the gyno's office. Luckily it was only a few minutes before he pulled into Jace's driveway.

Luc fumed silently in the driver's seat, not even bothering to cut the engine. Aiden hopped out and held his hand out to me.

I glanced at Luc. "Are you coming?"

"No. I'm going to the bar." His words were clipped, full of tension. Normally he'd never talk to me that way, but I gave him a pass considering everything that was going on.

"Okay." I slid out of the truck and followed Aiden into the house.

Skye and Arianna were sitting at the small kitchen table, a coffee mug in front of each of them.

"Thank goodness Luc found you," Skye said as she rushed over.

I raised both eyebrows. "Was I lost?"

"He said you weren't at home."

"I wasn't. I was with Aiden." I sat slumped down in her oversized plush chair and curled my feet under me. The wolf bite was taking its toll.

"Skye, I need to talk to you for a second," Aiden said, pulling her toward the front door.

The two of them spoke in hushed whispers,

making it impossible for me to hear what they were saying, but judging by the shocked expression on Skye's face as she spun to study me, it wasn't too hard to figure out. He'd told her about the mating.

That was fine. I would've told her myself if Arianna hadn't been in the room.

"Keep an eye on her," Aiden said. "We'll call as soon as we hear anything."

I bolted to my feet. "Where are you going?"

"To the bar with Luc. Jace is waiting for us." Aiden took two steps and stopped right in front of me. Caressing my cheek, he leaned down and brushed a faint kiss over my lips. "I'll be back as soon as I can. Then we can finish talking."

I jerked back and hastily glanced around, not at all used to the public display of affection.

"It's okay. They all know now," Aiden said

with a small smile. "Relax and get some rest."

Then he strode out, the door slamming closed behind him.

I stared at the door, longing for him to come back. The ache was so strong I was nearly compelled to chase after him. And that was something I definitely did not want to do. Not with Luc in the truck. I didn't have the energy to fight with him.

"It gets easier," Skye said.

"What does?"

"The connection. Right now your… ugh…" She glanced over at Arianna and lowered her voice again. "Your wolf craves him while you transition. It's normal."

I nodded, feeling as if someone had just ripped half my heart out. If I hadn't known it was so dangerous, I would've torn out of the house and walked to the bar if that was my only option. But if the Hunters really were here and had set the bar on fire, they weren't messing around. Wandering around at night would be worse than stupid.

Besides, I could barely keep my eyes open.

"Oh gosh. You need to lie down," Skye said, holding both hands out to me. "Come on. You can use my bed. Lord knows there's no way I'm getting any sleep until Jace walks back through that door and I'm certain he's completely whole."

Fierce protectiveness pierced my heart as I thought of Aiden and the others chasing down the Hunters. Not too long ago one of them had shot Luc in an attempt to gain control of the Riveaux land. Though why they wanted it, I wasn't entirely sure. The land was a sanctuary for wildlife. Even if they did gain control, it's not like they could develop it. It made no sense.

The Hunters were a small hate group who thought all shifters were dangerous, second-class citizens who needed to be wiped from the planet. Why they hadn't killed Luc when they had a chance was another mystery. Maybe the shooter just missed. Taking down a werewolf was not an easy feat. They heal too fast. But a bullet to the heart or head would usually do the trick.

A chill crept over me as foreboding settled deep in my gut.

"They'll be all right," Skye said softly as she tucked me in.

I stared up into her too-bright eyes and felt my heart sink. "You're going to have to try harder than that."

She sighed. "It's all I have right now."

Reaching out, I grabbed her hand. "Go sit with your friend. I'll be okay after I get some sleep."

"You'll be fine in the morning." She gave me a reassuring smile, then turned the light out and left me alone with my thoughts.

And all I could think about was Aiden running flat out in wolf form through the bayou, a group of gunmen at his heels.

CHAPTER 8

AIDEN

LUC FUMED BESIDE me in the truck as he took the corner too fast and sent the truck into a slide on the dirt road.

"Fuck!" Jerking the wheel, he managed to get the vehicle under control just before it fishtailed into a ditch.

"Feel better now?" I asked mildly.

"Shut up." He shot me a glare and tightened his grip on the wheel.

"Killing us both isn't going to help." I knew he was stressed about the bar and the Hunters, but this tantrum had everything to do with my involvement with Rayna.

"You're lucky to still be walking, *brother*." He turned onto the main highway that led to the bar and sped up. He kept his eyes glued to the road and spoke through clenched teeth. "Why her?"

His question pissed me off. "Why *not* her?"

"Because she's mine, dammit. That's why." His dark blue eyes flashed sapphire in the light as if he was moments from shifting.

I shook my head slowly. "No she isn't. She's not your mate. And never would've been. She's not your one. If she was, you would've already done something about it."

"You don't know that." His hands flexed against the steering wheel.

"Shit, Luc. Be honest with yourself. You've

been sharing that house with her for five years. Almost six now. Have you ever once even kissed her?" My gut tightened. The idea of my brother's hands on her stirred the primal animal in me.

His nostrils flared and I knew he sensed my wolf.

"Well, have you?" I demanded, my irritation building.

"I've thought about it," he said defensively.

"When?" Because he'd never once acted like she was more than a sister to him.

"When we were in high school."

I shook my head, disgusted. "She's not your fucking backup girl, Luc. Jesus Christ."

"I never—"

"Yes you did. You just told me she belongs to you. That no one else had the right to make a move. How else am I supposed to take that?"

We rounded a bend in the road and the bar came into view along with the lights of the fire truck and the sheriff's cruiser. Luc pulled into the lot, parked, and killed the engine.

Sitting back, he turned and met my judgmental stare. "She's my best friend, Aiden. I watch out for her. She was never supposed to become a were. I never wanted this life for her."

I couldn't necessarily blame him for that. We lived our lives under a veil of secrecy and were constantly being harassed by the likes of the Hunters. But he'd brought her into this long ago when he'd trusted her with our secret.

He reached for the door handle, but I placed my hand on his arm, stopping him, and said, "She was already one of us, part of our family, and would've been no matter what happened earlier tonight."

"That might be true," he said and shrugged me off. "But she doesn't have a choice now, does she?"

"No. She doesn't." Because there was no way I was letting her go now.

He let out a growl of disapproval and jumped out of the truck, slamming the door behind him.

My wolf settled, and despite the fact there'd been a fire at the bar, I felt more content than I had in months. Rayna was my mate, and even though Luc was pissed, he'd get over it soon enough. He'd have to.

Jace glowered at me when I finally joined him and Luc in front of the bar. "What took you so long?"

"He took Rayna home with him, and when

I got there they were showering. Together," Luc said.

Manny, the sheriff, cut his sharp gaze to me. "Rayna? Are you two… uh, together, or—"

"Yes," I snapped. "Now can we get back to the fire? What happened here?"

"Rayna?" Jace said, his brows raised in complete surprise. Then he glanced at Luc who stared straight ahead, ignoring us both.

"It just happened," I said.

"Right," Luc blurted, his tone full of sarcasm.

"Okay, enough." I raised my hands in the air as if to surrender. "Can we talk about that later? It looks like we have more pressing matters to attend to."

Jace nodded. "Right. Of course." He turned to Manny. "Can you give them the same run-down you just gave me? I need to go talk to the fire chief for a moment. Find out when we can get back in."

Manny nodded. "You got it."

Jace took off and disappeared behind the fire truck.

"Here." Manny handed me a copy of his report, but before I could take a look, Luc ripped it from my hands.

I ground my teeth together and let it go. It was too dark to read it anyway. "What happened?"

"Looks like arson. There was definitely an accelerant used. We found an empty gasoline can near the rear of the building along with footprints that lead toward the tree line. One of my guys tracked them into the woods, but there's nothing we can do until we get a couple of hounds out here at daybreak."

I turned to study the bar. "How bad is it? Do you know?"

He pressed his lips together, contemplating. "I only had a quick peek inside, but it looks like you boys will need a serious renovation before the fisherman around here can relax with a beer."

"Fuck!" Luc kicked the bottom step of the stairs leading to the porch.

"It's not good news, but insurance should probably cover it."

Even so, our income would take a serious hit. We had the swamp tours, but the bar was a good seventy-five percent of our gross.

"Any idea who did it?" I asked, not expecting an answer.

"My deputy saw someone peeling out of

here right before the fire alarm went off. He got me a car description and half a license plate number to go on. But that's it." He peered at us. "Anyone you can think of who'd want to do this? Any known enemies?"

Luc glanced at me, his expression stony. Of course we had an idea, but we couldn't tell the sheriff without divulging our wolf status. I shook my head and forced my lips up into an ironic smile. "Not unless Jace has a scorned old girlfriend. Now that Skye is permanently in the picture, his situation has changed. A lot."

Manny chuckled. "You can say that again. I thought I'd never see the day that boy settled down. But he sure did pick a looker."

Luc and I both nodded and let the conversation drop there.

"Well, we'll pick up that trail into the woods

at first light. If I had to guess, it's likely kids being idiots. But we'll get to the bottom of it soon enough."

I held my hand out to him. "Thanks for everything, Sheriff. We sure appreciate you coming out here in the middle of the night."

He slipped his hand into mine, his grasp firm. "No problem, boys. We'll be back at daybreak."

"Thanks," Luc said, giving him a nod.

The Sherriff tipped his hat and took off in his squad car, following the fire truck out of the lot.

Luc strode toward the back of the building without saying a word.

I swallowed my irritation and followed. We found Jace kneeling near the charred side of the building, his head tilted up as he scented the air.

"What is it?" I asked, turning to stare in the direction of the trees.

"They're still out there."

"The Hunters?" Luc asked, eyeing the broken window that led to the kitchen.

"Yes." Jace stood. "But they aren't over there." He pointed to the tree line where the sheriff said they'd seen tracks and then turned ninety degrees, his face etched with something close to fear. "They're that way."

"Your house," I said, my words barely audible.

"Shit!" Luc took off running first, followed quickly by Jace and me.

Our women were right in the line of fire.

CHAPTER 9

RAYNA

SWEAT TRICKLED DOWN my neck, pooling in my cleavage. Everything hurt. My joints, my eyes, my head. Even my teeth ached. Mild case of the flu, my ass. More like pneumonia. Or mono. Or the plague.

"Here." Skye sat on the side of the bed and pressed a mug into my hand. "This should help."

Heat radiated from the ceramic cup. I shook my head. "Too hot."

"It's root tea with ginger. It'll help." She

pressed a cool cloth to my brow.

"Okay," I croaked out and lifted my head.

She tipped the mug to my lips, and in my weakened state, only a fraction made it into my mouth. The rest spilled on her pillow. I swallowed what I could and flopped back down. "Sorry."

"Don't worry about it. I'll get you another pillow case."

I rolled over and curled into a ball, shivering from the fever.

And then pain exploded at my spine and my muscles spasmed, sending me into a fiery pit of confusion. My world spun. I knew nothing except the agony claiming every inch of my body. Bones crackled. Sounds intensified. Smells assaulted me. And I was overwhelmed with the faint trace of honey mixed with stale sweat and the undeniable tang of something that I inherently recognized as wolf.

Instincts took over and I jumped from the bed, landing easily on my newly formed four paws. My vision blurred as I barreled past Skye, through the bedroom, and straight into the kitchen to the back door. Jumping up, I hit the latch with one paw and the screen door flew open, enabling my escape to freedom.

My wolf was in complete control, carrying me straight into the cover of the bayou, the damp earth cooling my paws. All the pain had fled, replaced by euphoria. Mud mixed with wet bark and mildew filled my senses.

Run.

That word was my only coherent thought. Then suddenly a twig snapped, followed by a gunshot. Fear brought me to a sudden stop, and

I instinctively dropped to the ground, my ears twitching for any new sound.

"Get her!" a male voice shouted from the woods.

My hackles rose and I bared my teeth at the four men closing in, rifles pointed in my direction. I took one step forward and growled.

Trapped.

"Tranq her," the one in front of me said. "Now."

Snarling, I turned to the side and snapped at the closest man.

"Stupid bitch," he said and pointed his rifle at my head. "Do that again and your pelt will find a permanent home in front of my fireplace."

I froze, ice-cold fear bringing a clarity I hadn't had since my shift. I was wolf and these were the Hunters. They were far more likely to kill me in my wolf form than if I shifted back to human. Only then I'd be defenseless. And naked. Jesus. Why had I run from the cabin?

There was no real memory of intent. Just the shift and my wolf taking over. I had to get out of there. Away from them as soon as possible.

"Relax, Skye," the leader said, his voice soothing.

Oh, God. They thought I was Skye. They'd been after her.

"We only need you for a couple of days. Then, if you cooperate, you can get on with the rest of your life. Unless Billy over there has a use for you." His sinister laugh filled the small clearing, leaving me with no question as to what Billy would use me for. "He always talks about taking his bitches doggie style."

"Luscious blonde? Hell yeah, I have a use for her," the man who presumably was Billy said from behind me. "Maybe I'll make Riveaux watch."

My stomach rolled, and I had to suppress the urge to turn and rip his throat out. If I did, they'd shoot me for sure. I had to be calm. Try to wait them out until I saw an opportunity to flee.

"I bet you'd like Billy," the leader said with a laugh. "I've heard he's a fucking animal with the ladies."

An uncontrollable growl rumbled from the back of my throat.

The leader shook his head. "I told you to behave." He waved a hand and I heard the small click of a trigger followed by a sharp pain in my left front paw.

I yelped and danced around on three paws, catching sight of the tranq dart just before my world went black.

CHAPTER 10

AIDEN

J ACE SHIFTED IMMEDIATELY and ran off into the woods. Luc and I jumped into his truck and gunned it the few miles down the road to Jace's house. He was already there, still in wolf form and stalking the perimeter.

"What the fuck is he doing?" Luc scowled. "Arianna is in there. What if she sees him?"

"I doubt he cares much right now. The only thing on his mind is Skye and making sure she's all right."

But I knew as soon as I stepped out of the

truck that something was very wrong. Jace was in full-on wolf mode. The pack connection we shared was full of his anxiety and wolf aggression. He was ready for a fight. To tear someone limb from limb. Nothing would bring him back to his calm, measured demeanor except his mate. And she wasn't here. That much was clear. Otherwise she'd already be by his side.

Jace lifted his head, scented the air and took off once again into the woods of the bayou.

Rayna.

Following Luc, I raced up the steps and into the house. Arianna stood in the kitchen, her back to the pantry, clutching a cast-iron frying pan like it was a weapon.

"Ari?" Luc said softly. Moving slowly, he tentatively reached a hand out, being careful to not spook her further. "What happened here?"

Her almond-shaped eyes were wild with fear as she glanced between us.

"It's okay. Where's Skye?"

She pointed to the back door. "Followed the wolf."

I spun and ran into the bedroom. On the floor were the remnants of Rayna's tank top and her small skirt. "Dammit," I muttered. The shift had obviously taken her. Skye must've gone after her.

I strode back into the main room.

Arianna still held the frying pan, but her shoulders had slumped and tears stood in her eyes, though she hadn't allowed them to fall. "I don't understand. They were here and then…" She sucked in a breath and shook her head. "They…"

Luc pulled her into his arms and murmured

something in her ear.

"They're out there, Luc. We have to go," I said.

"Right behind you."

I nodded and moved toward the door.

"Stay here. Don't let anyone except one of us in," Luc said to Arianna.

"But Rayna, she was here and then she was just gone and the wolf—"

"I'll explain everything when we get back. Sit tight and don't worry. Everything's going to be fine." Luc gave her a quick hug and then joined me on the porch. "Shift?"

I shook my head, even though every fiber of my being was dying to do just that. Rayna was out there in wolf form, and I had to find her. But Jace and likely Skye had already shifted and were already tracking her. Someone needed to stay in human form. Wolves couldn't carry guns, which we'd need if we were going to battle the Hunters. "Not yet."

"Got it." He strode to the truck, opened the metal storage bin in the back of the bed, and pulled out his shotgun, two 9 mm handguns, and a hunting knife.

I joined him, took the knife, and hid it in my boot. Then he handed me one of the handguns and off we went, with Arianna watching us from the front window.

"She saw Rayna in wolf mode," I said.

"I know."

"You're probably going to have to tell her."

He shot me a what-the-fuck look. "Have you lost your mind? I just met her."

I shook my head. "She's going to be asking questions. Who knows what she saw when

Rayna shifted. And then Skye took off. It's better if we answer them rather than the sheriff or worse, one of the Hunters."

"Skye can take care of it," he said in a huff.

I eyed him. "Did you sleep with her?"

"Yeah. So?"

I gave him a flat stare. "It'll be better coming from you."

His grip tightened on the gun, and I had the distinct impression he'd like to bash me over the head with it. "Like you told Rayna what would happen to her after you bit her?"

That was enough. "Fuck off."

"That's what I thought you'd say." He picked up his pace and moved ahead of me.

I fumed behind him. The last thing I'd wanted to do was leave Rayna while she was going through the transition to a werewolf. And he damn well knew it. If the bar hadn't nearly burned to the ground, I wouldn't have.

We walked in near silence, listening to the night around us. Frogs croaked, crickets chirped, and unidentified birds whistled.

But as soon as we reached a small clearing, all sounds stopped and I knew we were close. Luc put his hand up to stop me, but I was already crouched down, checking for any signs of boot or pawprints. There, in the tiny sliver of moonlight peeking through the trees, was a fresh print—a large boot and, just to the right, one barely indented pawprint.

Jace. He'd already found their trail.

"That way." I pointed in the direction of the river. "They came by boat."

"The sheriff said he saw a car," Luc said.

"Maybe he did, but if the Hunters are still

here, they need some way to get out."

"All right. Assuming they are here, we need to get out of this clearing." Luc waved and I followed him into the canopy cover. We crept silently through the brush as we made our way toward the water's edge.

We'd only gone about twenty yards when I heard a yelp followed by a howl.

"Jace," we both said together and took off at a sprint.

Just before we cleared the tree line, Luc put his arm out, stopping me. I peered over his shoulder and spotted Jace still in wolf form, guarding a prone brindle-colored wolf who wasn't moving.

"It's Rayna," I said through clenched teeth.

Luc stiffened and raised his shotgun to his shoulder. "Is she okay?"

"She's breathing," was all I could get out. The agony in my chest, the kind you get when your heart is being ripped out, nearly brought me to my knees.

"I don't see Skye," Luc said, his voice so low I barely heard him.

I shook my head. I didn't see her either.

"Give up your mate, wolf," a tall, scruffy man said, waving his gun at Jace.

Mate?

Jace lowered his head and growled.

"Back off, Riveaux. Your girlfriend there fucked with the wrong people. That stunt she pulled a few weeks ago, threatening to out our creative business practices, didn't go unnoticed. Now the boss needs a word with her. And believe me when I say we aren't leaving without her."

Holy fuck. They thought Rayna was Skye. If they'd tracked her from Jace's house, that would make a certain amount of sense. No one knew Rayna had turned wolf except for us. The last time the Hunters had come around, they'd tried to blackmail us for our property. But Skye, who'd had no idea about the Hunter organization, used to live with one of their members and had come across two sets of books for her boyfriend's accounting business. Turns out he was laundering marijuana money for the Hunters. She'd threatened to turn them in if they didn't leave us alone.

Looks like they were calling her bluff. Except they had the wrong wolf.

I pulled the 9 mm from the back of my pants and leveled the gun at the Hunter that had a rifle pointed at Rayna.

"There's two more on the dock," I said, eyeing them as they pulled a line of rope from the bottom of their airboat.

"I see them." Luc turned and pointed his rifle at the ringleader. "Let's do this."

I nodded, and the pair of us slipped soundlessly from the trees.

CHAPTER II

RAYNA

I DON'T KNOW how long I was blacked out, but when I came to, Jace was standing in front of me, growling fiercely at the Hunters as they rambled on about taking me—well, Skye—to their drug boss. Guns were drawn. Tempers flared. And beneath it all, I sensed tension coming from Jace. It was a ball of unease in my chest that seemed inherently linked to him. A pack connection, I realized. Something primal. Uncontrollable. And completely welcome.

He was my family. Forever.

God, he was going to get himself killed protecting me. I couldn't let him do it. What about Skye? And Aiden and Luc?

Aiden. Strength filled my soul at the thought of him. Determination took over. This was not how my story would end.

Lying perfectly still, I watched Jace and two of the Hunters through slitted eyes. No one was paying attention to me. Both the Hunters were focused on Jace. Of course they were. Given the chance, he'd rip both of them to shreds.

And so would I.

I lay there for a few more moments and scanned the area, seeing nothing but darkness in the trees. Then I saw them. Brilliant bright blue eyes staring right at me from under a bush only a few feet away.

Skye. She was here. We were now three

against four, though from my vantage point, I couldn't tell where the other two Hunters were.

We needed a distraction.

Movement came from the woods, and then as if I'd conjured them up, Aiden and Luc appeared from the cover of the trees.

"Drop the gun, asshole," Aiden said, training his weapon on the slightly overweight man nearest to me.

The leader spun and aimed his gun in the direction of Luc's chest. But Luc was too fast for him and brought his shotgun down on the guy's forearm, making him drop the gun as he fell to one knee.

I leaped, aiming straight for the pudgy man's throat. But I wasn't yet used to my wolf body and overshot the distance, catching him in the face with my back paws. We both went down, and I landed in a heap a few feet away, instantly scrambling to get back up.

"Billy!" my victim called. "Take care of this bitch!"

I spun to find Billy coming straight for me, that tranq gun aimed at me again. But before he could get a shot off, Skye pounced and caught his wrist in her vicious jaws.

Growling my approval, I ran past her, cutting off the fourth Hunter before he could get into the mix.

Shouts and howls sounded behind me in the fight, but I was focused. Take down the Hunter.

A shot rang out, and I froze as a bullet zinged past me, followed by another and a blinding white heat that tore through my back right leg.

Howling, I tucked the leg under, turned, and ran full speed at the shooter. It was Billy, the would-be rapist. He'd gotten away from Skye and was still pointing that gun at me.

"Don't make me shoot you again. I don't want you too banged up before we have our fun later." The sneer on his face only fueled my hate.

"Rayna!" Aiden shouted.

It was just enough to break Billy's concentration. But not mine. I jumped and this time caught him in the gut as I sank my jaws into his shoulder. We fell to the ground, him grabbing my neck and punching the side of my head.

I felt nothing but his hot blood pouring over my tongue.

The salty tang of it drove my wolf to a state of frenzy. He was my prey.

My kill.

"Rayna!" Aiden's voice penetrated the bloodlust haze and reality came rushing back.

The man beneath me had stilled.

I froze, then let go and jumped off of him, gagging.

"It's all right," Aiden said, dropping his hand to the top of my head. "Everything's all right now."

I heard the faint sound of the airboat in the distance and the low murmur of voices.

"Rayna?"

I turned my head and stared into Skye's now-human face. She'd shifted back and was wearing a green button-down shirt that came to midthigh.

"You should shift back now. You're safe. It'll help you heal."

Heal? Oh, right. The bullet had grazed one of my legs. I moved my head from side to side. I couldn't shift in front of everyone. And where were the Hunters? I twisted and spotted Jace, who was buck naked, standing over two of them. Luc, who was now shirtless, was restraining them with rope. That's where Skye had gotten her shirt. The other two were nowhere to be found.

"I'll take care of her," Aiden said to Skye. "You and Jace go and call the sheriff."

She nodded and left to join Jace. A few seconds later, they were both back in wolf form and running back toward their house.

Aiden peeled his shirt off and kneeled beside me. "Skye's right, baby. I need you to shift now. You'll never make it back to the truck on that leg in wolf form."

I stared into his worried eyes and felt the panic ripple through me. How in the world was I supposed to initiate a shift? It had just happened last time. Closing my eyes, I visualized shifting back to my human form. I should be able to do this. I'd seen Luc do it a million times. He would concentrate and then just like that, he'd shift. Only it wasn't happening for me. There was no pull or magic. Just me standing there thinking about being human again.

A fresh wave of panic took over. What if I never got back? Oh, God. I was going to be a wolf for the rest of my life.

"Ray," Aiden said softly. "Relax. You're way too tense."

A whine escaped my throat as I lay down, resting my head on my paws.

"Don't give up. We need to get you home."

I rolled my head to the side and stared off into the bayou. Putting pressure on me wasn't going to help.

He let out a small sigh of resignation and proceeded to divest himself of his jeans. "Okay, then. If you can't shift to human, I'll shift to wolf."

I jerked my head up and watched in awe as he transformed from my beautiful, glorious man to a pure silver wolf.

"Aiden," Luc said, impatience in his tone. "You don't have time for this. The sheriff is on his way."

Aiden ignored him and lay down right next to me. His big wolf head pressed up against me, and I had the feeling everything was going to be okay. I had my mate. My muscles started to relax and my lids got heavy with sleep. I could pass out right then and there except for the fact that the adrenaline had worn off and my leg was starting to throb.

Crap. Aiden was right. I had to shift. The leg hurt too much.

Now that Aiden was snuggled up to me, I had the sense that I was closer to my wolf than I had been before, almost as if we were a partnership instead of two separate parts fighting for control like when I'd shifted in Skye's bedroom. I felt as if I could accomplish anything. Like I was strong.

Sucking in a breath, I focused this time on the memory of being held in Aiden's arms. To being kissed so thoroughly by him.

A tug pulled from deep in my gut, and then I was pulled into a mental spiraling vortex as my vision blurred. The shift took over, reforming my wolf body into my human state. This time wasn't nearly as painful... Well, except for my leg. But the rest wasn't so bad. That was until I found myself sitting naked in the dirt.

Yuck. I pushed myself up, surprised to find my leg was only slightly sore. Dang, the shift really had helped.

More than a little mortified to be naked in front of Luc, I reached down and grabbed the T-shirt Aiden had been wearing and pulled it over my head. By the time my head popped out of the top, Aiden was standing in front of me with a self-satisfied smile.

"There you are, gorgeous." He cupped my cheek and brushed his fingers down to my jawline.

"Put your pants on," Luc barked from the pier.

Aiden gave him a sideways glance.

I chuckled. "He's modest."

"He's not in the least, and you know it." Aiden turned and picked up his discarded jeans. Once he was dressed again, he held his hand out to me. "Let's go. We need to get you out of here."

I glanced back at Luc. "We're just going to leave him here?"

"Yes," Luc called.

"No," I called back. "Two of them got away, didn't they?"

"Yes, but they won't be back tonight. Not when their buddies are being taken away for arson." He turned and gave me a pained look. "Go home with Aiden. I'll see you sometime tomorrow."

I glanced up at Aiden. "Can I have just a

minute with him before we go?"

He nodded. "Make it quick. I really do want you far from here when the sheriff arrives."

"Got it." I limped over to Luc.

He stood facing the water, his arms crossed over his chest.

"Want to talk about it?" I asked.

"What's to talk about? You shagged my brother and then he bit you. End of story."

"That's not all," I said, irritated by his attitude. "I asked him to bite me. Demanded it in fact. I chose this. Nothing was forced on me. So get over it. I knew what I was doing when I chose this life. You should be happy for me."

"Happy that you used my brother to turn were?" he yelled. "Jesus, Rayna, if you wanted this life that badly, you could've asked me years ago."

I took a step back, feeling as if I'd been slapped. "What does that mean? I could've asked you?"

"Exactly what I said. I would've bitten you if it meant that much to you."

I let out a loud huff and advanced on him, my hands on my hips. "You're a real piece of work, you know that? You'd have bitten me. God, Luc. You'd have made me your mate just so someone else couldn't?"

"That's not—"

"Don't even try it. Listen and listen carefully to what I have to say."

He gave a noncommittal shrug that pissed me off even more. Damn him.

"Fine. Here's the deal. I asked Aiden to bite me because I wanted to be Aiden's mate. Not yours. Contrary to popular belief, I was not hanging around waiting for you to make up your mind about us. That was never an option. And we both know that."

Luc stared at the water. "I just meant we'd have found a way to get you what you wanted."

"You don't understand," I said, leaning in to give him a kiss on the cheek. "I'm already getting everything I need and want." I met Aiden's fiery gaze. "And I wanted to mate with Aiden, not just use him for his bite. I'd never do that. And I hope you can see that. If not, we bloody well might still have a problem here."

"You wanted… Aiden?"

"That's right, little brother," Aiden said, joining us. "And I wanted to mate with her."

Luc shifted his gaze between us and narrowed his eyes in suspicion. "How long?"

"How long what?" I asked, confused.

"How long have you been together?" Luc pierced me with a stare. "And why didn't you tell me?"

I stepped up to him and placed my hand on his chest, over his heart. "I know this threw you for a loop. It did me too. And I didn't tell you because I wasn't sure it was going anywhere. There was no reason to upset you if things didn't work out."

"About three years now," Aiden said from behind us.

I spun. "What?"

He gave us a shy smile. "I've been thinking about what it would be like to have you in my bed for longer than that. Since you were about sixteen actually." He tore his gaze from me and focused on Luc. "But I never did anything about it because I always thought of her as your girl. Until now."

Aiden held his hand out to me.

I gaped at him. "You've wanted me as your mate for *three* years?"

He nodded, his expression going soft with affection. "Yes. I've known, but haven't been willing to admit it to myself. I couldn't even let myself go there. But then tonight…" Heat flashed in his eyes. "You asked me to, and there was no turning you down."

Joy spilled through me and tears stung my eyes. "Then you didn't lose control."

He shook his head and pulled me to him.

Luc cleared his throat. "I hate to interrupt this oh-so-touching moment. But you two have to get out of here."

I let go of Aiden and turned to Luc, searching his expressionless gaze. "Are we okay?"

A muscle in his jaw twitched. But then he let out a slow breath and dropped the hardened attitude. Emotion filtered through is dark blue eyes, and he pulled me to him, hugging me. "Yeah, Ray. We're good. You know I only want you to be happy, and if Aiden's the one, then I'm fine with it. Or will be once I get used to it."

I pulled back and smiled at him. "He is."

"Okay. But if he doesn't treat you right..." Luc shot Aiden a warning glance.

I tensed, but Aiden chuckled.

"If I fuck up, I fully expect you to take me down, brother," Aiden said to Luc. "I think we both know Rayna deserves better than the likes of me, but she's stuck with me now. And I'll do my damnedest to do right by her."

"You got that right." Luc bent and brushed a light kiss over my cheek and whispered,

"Welcome to the family, Ray."

I blinked and a single tear fell.

Luc gently brushed it away with his thumb. "Nothing's going to change. You're still my best girl. Got it?"

I nodded. "I love you, you big jerk."

"I know. Now get out of here. Both of you."

Aiden wrapped his arm around me, and the pair of us disappeared into the trees.

"You think he'll really be okay?" I asked Aiden.

"Sure. We wolves are pretty territorial, and even though you two haven't ever been romantic, he's always been your wolf. Now I am. He'll adjust."

"I hope so," I said, still worried.

"Trust me. When he finds his fated mate, he'll understand."

I stopped dead in my tracks. "Fated mate?"

He frowned at me. "What's wrong?"

"Nothing. I… Whoa, okay. Are you saying I'm your fated mate? Because that's what it sounded like, and I don't want to misunderstand if that's not what you meant."

"Ray," he said, his voice low and full of something that could only be described as love. "Yes, I'm saying you're my fated mate. You're my one and only one. I don't want you to ever think I was pushed or tricked into mating with you. I wanted you. Hell, I *want* you. Always. I wouldn't have bitten you otherwise."

"Oh, God," I said softly and melted into him.

His arms tightened around me, and we stood there in the darkness for a moment, just holding each other.

"You're mine," I whispered.

"Yours," he agreed.

"Then take me home. To your home."

"Our home."

CHAPTER 12

AIDEN

EVEN THOUGH RAYNA and I had only been mated for about a week, it was hard for me to recall a time when we weren't together. I felt as if she'd always been a part of me. In a way she had, but not like this.

"Aiden, get dressed. They'll be here any moment," Rayna said from the doorway of the bathroom.

I grinned at her from the bed, still completely naked after our midafternoon lovemaking session.

"Stop." She laughed and tugged her long dark locks up into a full ponytail. "If your junk is still hanging out when they get here, I'm going to steal your clothes and make you barbeque in your birthday suit."

My grin widened. "It's nothing they haven't all seen before."

She rolled her eyes. "Just get dressed. Skye's model friends are coming over. No need to scandalize them."

I rolled off the bed and made my way to the bathroom, catching her around the waist. "What if I want to make you come again, just one more time?"

A blush crept up her neck and stained her cheeks. She bit her lip, and I knew she was considering it. But then she pulled away and shook her head, giving me her no-nonsense glare. "Stop distracting me. They'll be here in—"

A knock sounded on the door.

"Shoot. That's them!" She ran from the bedroom and called over her shoulder, "Hurry up."

Pleased and more content than I'd ever been, I shut myself in the bathroom and took a quick shower. Rayna was more than capable of entertaining our family without me. Hell, she'd been a part of it for twenty years now. Only now she had a different role as my mate.

And for all our worrying, everyone had accepted it. It was obvious Luc was still having a bit of an issue with letting her go, but he was trying. And that was enough.

He'd not only taken care of making sure the two Hunters we'd apprehended had been hauled off to jail where they belonged, but he'd also sent out word that if the other two ever showed up on our property, he'd shoot first and dump their bodies, no questions asked.

As far as a threat went, I was fully on board. They'd nearly killed Rayna, and neither of us was going to let that slide. We'd bonded over the plan one night last week after we'd both had one too many drinks. It was then I'd known we really would be okay.

Dressed in fresh jeans and T-shirt, I emerged from the house to find Jace already grilling the steaks and Skye taking photos of Rayna, Arianna, and two of her other model friends down by the river.

Luc was sitting on an old tree stump, a beer in hand, watching them intently.

I sat next to him, content to watch Rayna laughing at something Skye had said. Warmth filled my chest, the feeling I'd come to recognize as love.

"What's it like?" Luc asked.

I turned, my eyebrows raised in surprise. Outside of the night we'd gotten shitfaced and agreed we'd murder anyone who laid a hand on Rayna, we hadn't spoken much all week. "What's what like?"

He kept his gaze trained straight ahead. "Being mated. Is it worth it?"

His question was completely unexpected, and it took me a moment to form a reply. "Yeah. It's different than I thought. I guess I used to think if I mated with someone, I'd feel like I had an anchor weighing me down. Like my freedom would be lost or something. But really it's the opposite. Rayna makes me feel lighter. Freer somehow. Like everything is right for once and nothing's missing."

He turned to me, his eyes flashing with irritation. "I know, you jackass. She's been my best friend for twenty years. With her everything is better. That's what being around an amazing person does for you."

"It's not the same," I said, fighting the urge to deck him. "Mates are different."

He let out a huff of laughter. "No kidding. But that's not what I meant when I asked if it was worth it. I want to know that if everything goes to shit, that if she leaves you like Mom left us, would it still be worth it? Would you mate with her again?"

Jesus. All of this was about our mother. She was the reason he'd held on to Rayna for so long, had never let himself get close to anyone else. Why he hadn't wanted a mate. Everything suddenly clicked into place.

Turning my gaze to the one who now held my heart in her hands, I nodded. "Yes. It's worth it."

Luc let out a breath, nodded, and stood up. "That's what I thought you'd say."

Then he strode over to the girls and pulled Arianna from the lineup. The two stood by the water's edge talking, until suddenly he took her in his arms and kissed her so thoroughly that by the time he let her up, her face was flushed and her eyes a little unfocused.

Rayna stared, her mouth open, shocked by Luc's out-of-character behavior. But then she clasped her hands together and let out a wolf whistle of appreciation.

The others joined in, and everyone laughed when Luc invited Arianna to take a bow.

With a smile lighting up her face, Rayna

crossed the yard and sat on my lap. She wrapped her arm around my neck and said, "Looks like he's doing all right."

"I would say so." I ran my fingers up the inside of her thigh, stopping at the hem of her impossibly short shorts. "But I'm not. You're killing me in these, Ray."

She dipped her head down and brushed her lips over mine. "That's the plan."

I groaned and caught her lips in a searing kiss. When I released her, her breath was short and her eyes were full of lust.

I got up, gently placing her on her feet, and whispered in her ear. "I just wanted to know that you're wet and waiting for me."

"Damn wolf," she muttered and turned into me again. "You're impossible, you know that?"

I grinned. "You could always ask them to

leave."

"Shut up." Laughing, she rose up on her tip-toes and kissed the corner of my mouth. Then she whispered, "When they do leave, what exactly is it you want to do to me?"

My body tensed with anticipation, and I opened my mouth to fill her ear with all my dirty thoughts, but she placed two fingers to my lips, stopping me.

"No, I think I'd rather you keep it to your-self until later." Then she gave me a saucy smile and sauntered off toward the water. Pausing, she turned and glanced over her shoulder. "Coming?"

Damn straight I was. As often as possible.

Sign up for Kenzie's newsletter at www.kenziecox.com to be notified of new releases. Do you prefer text messages? Sign up for text alerts! Just text SHIFTERSROCK to 24587 to register.

Book List:

<u>Wolves of the Rising Sun</u>

Jace

Aiden

Luc

Craved

Silas

Darien

Wren

Printed in Great Britain
by Amazon